a. Loock out
B. o.u.t

C. T. E.
16. B. A.
99. B.
12. C.
B.

Walt Disney

Mickey's Christmas Carol

Twin Books

One Christmas Eve long ago it snowed very hard in London. A thick blanket of snow covered the roofs and window sills, and the carriage wheels left tracks in the streets. Gently falling snowflakes tickled the townsfolk hurrying homeward, laden with Christmas gifts.

But one person was not thinking about Christmas trees nor presents. He paid no attention to the gaily decorated houses — for his name was Ebenezer Scrooge!

Ebenezer Scrooge hurried past a group of carolers.

"Joy to children far and near,

What a wondrous time of year," they sang.

"God bless you, sir," one of them called out. "Please spare a coin for a poor, hungry child!"

"Bah! Humbug!" replied Scrooge. "Stand aside there — I have no time to dawdle. Not a penny will you get from me! If the poor want to be rich then let them work as hard as I do."

With his cane Scrooge angrily knocked the snow from the sign above his office door. He was thinking about his partner, Jacob Marley, who had passed away seven years ago that very night.

"He was a good one! He robbed the widows and swindled the poor! In his will he left me enough money to pay for his tombstone — and I had him buried at sea! Ha, ha!" Scrooge chuckled to himself.

Even though it was Christmas Eve, Scrooge's clerk, Bob Cratchit, was busily working. He had been copying letters all day, and although he wore a scarf and gloves, his teeth were chattering loudly.

"A-A-CHOO!" sneezed Cratchit. "It's freezing today. Surely Scrooge won't miss one little piece of coal." Cratchit carefully lifted the coal bucket, but did not see who was coming up the sidewalk.

9

Suddenly Scrooge burst into the room. He tossed his bag of dirty laundry on the floor and waved his cane in the air.

"Caught you!" he shouted at Cratchit. "Are you trying to ruin me? That coal costs a pretty penny, you know."

"Heh, heh," stammered Cratchit. "I was just trying to thaw my ink."

"Bah! You used a piece last week," the miserly Scrooge replied. "Now get back to work!"

Old Scrooge sat down at his desk and lovingly polished his gold coins until they glowed brightly.

Rubbing his hands together with glee, he weighed the coins on the scales and stacked them carefully on the desktop. With a quill pen, he scratched figures in an enormous book. Suddenly the door flew open with a bang.

"Merry Christmas!" someone cried. Cratchit looked up from his work and gave a hearty greeting to Scrooge's nephew Fred, who stood in the doorway, grinning broadly.

"What's this, Uncle Scrooge?" Fred exclaimed. "Poor Cratchit still working on Christmas Eve?"

"Bah! Humbug!" snorted Scrooge. "We never close!" Bob Cratchit looked sadly at his ledger.

"Christmas, a *humbug?*"
asked Fred in disbelief. "Why,
surely you don't mean it,
Uncle. Will you dine with us
tomorrow?"

"What? Never!" replied
Scrooge. "A year older and no
richer — I have no reason to
be merry."

"Then take this wreath as a
sign of friendship," said his
nephew.

Scrooge snatched the wreath
and threw it into the fire.
"Now good day to you, sir,
there is work to be done,"
Scrooge said rudely.

Fred tipped his hat and left,
giving Cratchit a look of pity.

"Oh, to spend Christmas Day at home," thought Cratchit as he stepped down wearily from his stool.

"Not so fast, it's not quite seven o'clock," snapped Scrooge. "And I suppose you will be wanting tomorrow off?"

"Why, yes. Yes," stammered Cratchit in amazement.

"Then mind you are in even earlier the day after, and don't forget my dirty laundry!"

Cratchit snatched up the bag of laundry and was gone in an instant, shouting a "Merry Christmas!" as he went.

Scrooge locked up his office and hurried home through the swirling snow. As he climbed the dark, steep steps he took an old key from his pocket.

Suddenly Scrooge took a closer look at his door-knocker. Then he gasped.

"Am I seeing things? No, it couldn't be . . . Jacob Marley? Is that you?"

The face on the door called softly, "Scrooooooge!"

Frightened, Scrooge yanked open the door, ran inside, and slammed the door behind him.

Scrooge flew up the stairs three at a time, but behind him he could hear the sound of chains clanking.

Looking over his shoulder, he froze in his tracks. The ghost of Marley had come back to haunt him!

Scrooge ran into his bedroom and slammed the door shut. In a jiffy it was locked and bolted.

"That's it — no ghost can get through that," he said, trying to convince himself. But in the dark shadows of his gloomy apartment, Scrooge shivered. The dust sheet on his chair fluttered and made him jump.

Clink . . . Clank . . . Clink . . . Clank . . . The chains dragged closer.

Scrooge sank down in his chair, his teeth clacking like
castanets. He knew that no door had ever kept a ghost out
— although this ghost knocked politely before he floated in.
    "Scrooge, don't you recognize your old friend?" asked
the ghost. "I was your partner, Jacob Marley."

Suddenly a great rattling of chains could be heard as the ghost tripped over Scrooge's cane. His legs shot into the air and he landed in a heap on the floor. Then a deafening thud shook the room as a heavy chest fell beside him.

Scrooge, his fright forgotten, shot from his chair. "Hah! Hah! You don't fool me," he said. "The real Jacob Marley was never so clumsy."

"Silence! Do not mock me!" boomed the ghost. "If I am clumsy, 'tis because of these chains I must always carry with me."

"What about that chest?" exclaimed Scrooge. "Hand over the keys, Marley. Let me take a look."

"Stop!" thundered the ghost. "Not so fast, old man. This chest is heavier than all the treasure in the world. All my miserable deeds are locked in here, and chained to me forever. I can never be free." The ghost shook his chains fiercely, then continued, "I come to warn you, Scrooge. Change your ways or you are doomed!" Marley raised his hand and Scrooge's knees began knocking together.

33

The ghost was not finished. "You will be visited this night by three spirits," he said. "Do not send them away. Listen to them well, for only they can save you now." In an instant Marley was gone, and only the faint *Clink! Clank!* of chains could be heard.

Scrooge stood for a moment in a daze, then he quickly pulled on his nightshirt and cap, hopped into bed, and pulled the covers right up to his nose. He wondered if it had been a dream, and was almost asleep when a dark shadow appeared on the wall. He had another visitor.

Out of the shadows stepped a little figure with a top hat on his head and an umbrella under his arm.

"The hour has come, Mr. Scrooge!" he called. "Hurry! There is not a moment to lose."

"But . . . but . . . who are you?" croaked Ebenezer.

"I am the Ghost of Christmas Past," the figure replied. "Do as I say."

"A midget!" snickered Scrooge. "Go away! You do not frighten me."

"Silence!" ordered the Spirit. "If men were measured by their kindness, you would be smaller than a grain of sand!"

"Catch hold of my coattails," commanded the Spirit, "for we are going back to a time when Christmas was not *humbug!*" Scrooge hesitated, but remembering Marley's terrible warning, he grasped the Spirit and held on tightly.

The window flew open, and instantly Scrooge and the Spirit of Christmas Past soared over rooftops and chimneys, the Spirit's red umbrella keeping them afloat. Scrooge's nightshirt fluttered in the chilly breeze.

They came to a stop outside a brightly lit house. Peering through the window, Scrooge couldn't believe his eyes.

"Why, it's Isabelle!" he cried, remembering suddenly the girl he'd once loved. "But who is that she is dancing with so merrily?"

"That man was you, Scrooge," whispered the Spirit, "in the days when you, too, were kind and cheerful." They gazed through the window a moment longer; then the Spirit whisked Scrooge away to another scene.

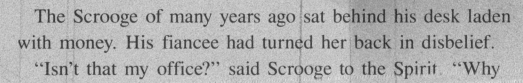

The Scrooge of many years ago sat behind his desk laden
with money. His fiancee had turned her back in disbelief.
"Isn't that my office?" said Scrooge to the Spirit. "Why
is Isabelle crying?"
The Spirit gave Scrooge a withering look, and
suddenly Scrooge remembered. He had foreclosed
on her cottage, and lost Isabelle forever.

The Spirit turned from the window. "Your greed drove her away, Ebenezer. You were to marry, but you loved only money."

"No, no . . ." moaned Scrooge. "Isabelle! I wanted us to be happy . . . to be rich . . ."

"You left her with nothing!" accused the Spirit.

"Oh, please, Spirit," groaned Scrooge. "I cannot bear these memories. Take me home!"

"You fashioned those memories yourself, Scrooge," the Spirit said sternly.

Suddenly Scrooge found himself once more in his bed. "That couldn't have happened," he thought. "I couldn't have flown through the air. That was just a bad dream." Then he thought of Isabelle, and how his love of money had ruined his chance for happiness with the girl he had loved.

Only the lonely *tick! tock!* of the clock could be heard.

Scrooge was sobbing into
his pillow when he felt a
heavy hand on his shoulder.
   "I am the Ghost of
Christmas Present!" boomed a
fierce-looking giant.
   "Oh, please!" cried
Scrooge. "Spare me."

The Giant picked up Scrooge by his nightshirt and examined him very closely.

"Hah! Hah!" he chortled. "So this is the rogue who swindles ladies. See if your money will help you now!"

"No! Don't hurt me, please! Have mercy — take my treasure — you can have it all!"

"Keep your treasure, Scrooge, it is of no use to me," the giant Spirit replied. "Money cannot buy happiness, and only my generosity can save you now. Have a grape, why don't you?" With that, the Spirit took an enormous bunch of grapes from his pocket and dropped Scrooge onto it none too gently. Slipping and sliding, Scrooge called out for help, but the Spirit just laughed.

"I have the power to give you life, but what have you ever given? Let us take a look."

"There's no time to lose," the Spirit cried, scooping up Scrooge and putting him in his pocket. He pushed open the roof and stepped out, as though from a doll's house. His big red nose glowed brightly in the dark night.

"At least it's warm in here," Scrooge murmured as he peeked out of the pocket. "But I wonder where we are going."

In seconds the Spirit and Scrooge had arrived at a tiny, run-down house.

"What a dreadful little house!" exclaimed Scrooge, looking in the window. "Who could live in such a place? Perhaps a miserable beggar?"

"Look closer, Scrooge," advised the Spirit, "tell me who you see."

Scrooge pressed his face against the glass for a better look. "Why, it's Bob Cratchit, my clerk!" he said with surprise. "Does he live *here*?"

The Spirit scowled. "Look how he lives, thanks to your generosity! Look at the food his family must eat this Christmas Eve because it's all they can afford."

The hungry Cratchit family sat at their table, about to carve up the smallest goose Scrooge had ever seen in his life.

"That's a very tiny goose," he commented, "but what is in that huge pot on the stove?"

"That, Mr. Scrooge, is your laundry!" said the Spirit. Scrooge hid his face in shame.

As Scrooge watched, a small boy hobbled into the room, leaning on a little crutch.

"Who is that boy, and why does he walk so slowly?" asked Scrooge.

"That is Tiny Tim," replied the Spirit. "He will soon be one less mouth for the family to feed."

"Yippee! It's a goose — what a treat!" Tiny Tim cried.

"But where is Tiny Tim going?" Scrooge asked fearfully.

"Tiny Tim is very sick. He must have good food every day to make him well again," said the Spirit. And as they watched the frail boy's joyful face, a tear rolled down the Giant's cheek.

Suddenly the scene shifted, and although the Spirit and Scrooge were looking in the same window, it was a later time.

"What's wrong?" asked Scrooge. "Where is Tiny Tim? Why are the Cratchits crying?"

Suddenly the churchbells began to toll, and Scrooge knew, even though the Spirit didn't answer his question, that poor Tiny Tim was dead.

When Scrooge stepped back from the window, the Spirit had disappeared. A smoky haze hung in the air. Shivering, Scrooge was almost blown into the air by a gust of freezing wind.

"Help! H-E-L-P!" he called. "Don't leave me here . . . . Come back!" The swirling smoke was much thicker now.

Scrooge sneezed so hard that he went flying through the air, then landed with a thud in some deep, soft snow.

"W-w-w-where am I, and why are there so many tombstones?" he wondered. But Scrooge was no longer alone. A horrible specter, his face as black as soot, stood silently before him.

The Spirit took off his hood, and Scrooge saw what had made him sneeze: a gigantic cigar glowed in the Spirit's horrible mouth. Suddenly he spoke. "I am the Ghost of Christmas Yet to Come. Who are you looking for in this lonely place?"

"Please sir, help me find Tiny Tim," begged Scrooge. Very slowly the Spirit raised his hand and pointed to a tombstone.

Scrooge looked, and saw Bob Cratchit placing Tiny Tim's little crutch on a grave. Tears rolled down Cratchit's face.

Scrooge's heart sank. He wanted to say how sorry he was, when suddenly the bell began to toll once more.

Scrooge turned away, tears in his eyes. He saw another grave gaping in front of him. "Who — whose lonely grave is this?" he asked the Ghost of Christmas Yet to Come.

"Why, yours, Ebenezer," laughed the Spirit, lighting another cigar.

Scrooge peered anxiously
into the dark hole, but he
could see nothing. "Oh,
please!" he cried. "I'm so
sorry! Tell me these events
can yet be changed!"

But the Spirit just laughed, and
slapped Scrooge on the back.

"H-e-e-e-l-p!" screamed Scrooge, as he went flying into the pit.

As he fell, he remembered all the people he had robbed and swindled in the past.

"I'll change! Let me out! Let me . . ."

Suddenly another bell could be heard. Scrooge opened his eyes, and with utter joy he found himself in his own bed. "Hooray!" he shouted, with tears of happiness rolling down his cheeks. "My own bed," he said lovingly.

He jumped up and ran to the window. The sun shone brightly, and the bells were ringing. It was Christmas morning.

"But, but, if it is still Christmas morning," stammered Scrooge, "what the Spirit showed me last night has not yet happened. Tiny Tim still lives!"

Scrooge threw on his hat
and coat and ran outside.
"There's not a moment to
lose. I've a lot to do and it
won't wait!"

"Merry Christmas!" the
carolers called to Scrooge.

"And a Merry Christmas to
you!" replied Scrooge. The
carol singers could not believe
their luck as Scrooge pushed
gold coins into their hands.

"Merry Christmas, Fred!" Scrooge cried to his nephew. "I've no time to stop, but don't start dinner without me! There's just one thing I must do. Mind you cook the turkey just how I like it, and don't forget the chestnuts!"

Fred was so surprised at his uncle's cheerfulness, he almost fell off his carriage.

Rat! Tat! Tat! Bob Cratchit heard a sharp knock on his
door, and ran to open it. Tiny Tim wasn't far behind.

Cratchit's face fell when he saw who was standing on the
step: it was Scrooge, with a big brown sack on his back.
He looked very cross.

"Why, Mr. Scrooge, what do you want?" Bob
stammered.

Scrooge pointed his cane at Cratchit. "As you're not
working today, I've brought a sack of dirty laundry," he
said. "See that it is done today!"

Mrs. Cratchit stepped forward, her lip trembling as she spoke. "Surely not on Christmas Day, Mr. Scrooge," she said.

"Oh! Look!" cried Tiny Tim to his sister as Scrooge walked past. "Isn't that a teddy bear in Mr. Scrooge's pocket?" Tiny Tim reached out his hand . . .

. . . just as Scrooge swung around. He looked very angry,
but instead of boxing Tiny Tim's ears, he threw the sack
on the floor. "Open it!" he cried.

Parcels tied with bright ribbons and bows tumbled from
the sack. Scrooge laughed as the children's faces lit up
with joy. Tiny Tim and his sister carried the gifts to the
Christmas tree to open them.

"Oh! It's a drum!" cried the girl. "Just what I always wanted!"

"It's a rocking horse! God bless you, Mr. Scrooge!" cried Tiny Tim, running over to give him a big hug.

"There are more surprises, children," chuckled Scrooge. "Look at the marvelous goose, and there are chestnuts and even a Christmas pudding! What a Christmas you shall have." Scrooge looked at Cratchit, and continued, "A very Merry Christmas to you all, and especially to *you*, Tiny Tim!" Scrooge gave the boy a wink.

The whole family danced with joy. This was to be the first of many bountiful holidays, for they would never be poor again. Cratchit was to become Scrooge's new partner, and Tiny Tim wouldn't go hungry, and would grow stronger each day.

And Ebenezer Scrooge, seeing their smiling faces, felt very, very happy indeed. "How good it is to be generous and kind!" he thought.

"God bless us, every one," said Tiny Tim.

Published by
Penguin Books USA Inc.,
375 Hudson Street
New York, New York, 10014

Produced by
Twin Books
15 Sherwood Place
Greenwich, CT 06830

© 1988 The Walt Disney Company

Reprinted in 1992

ISBN 0-453-03015-7

Printed in Hong Kong

10 9 8 7 6 5 4 3 2